The First Day of Winter

For Will, Jane, and Ian

H SQUARE FISH

Imprints of Macmillan
175 Fifth Avenue
New York, NY 10010
mackids.com

Henry Holt® is a registered trademark of Macmillan Publishing Group, LLC.
Publishers since 1866.
Square Fish and the Square Fish logo are trademarks of Macmillan and
are used by Henry Holt and Company under license from Macmillan.

Square Fish books may be purchased for business or promotional use.
For information on bulk purchases, please contact the Macmillan Corporate
and Premium Sales Department at (800) 221-7945 x5442 or by e-mail at
specialmarkets@macmillan.com.

The illustrations were created using colored cotton fiber, hand-cut stencils, and squeeze bottles.
Book design by Denise Fleming and David Powers. Visit denisefleming.com.

Library of Congress Cataloging-in-Publication Data
Fleming, Denise.
The first day of winter / Denise Fleming.
Summary: A snowman comes alive as the child building it adds
pieces during the first ten days of winter.
ISBN 978-0-8050-7384-3 (hardcover)
ISBN 978-0-312-37138-8 (paperback)
[1. Snowmen—Fiction. 2. Counting. 3. Stories in rhyme.] I. Title.
PZ8.3.F6378Fi 2005
[E]—dc22   2004022181

Originally published in the United States by Henry Holt and Company
First Square Fish Edition: 2012
Square Fish logo designed by Filomena Tuosto
F&P: I

ISBN 978-0-8050-7384-3   (Henry Holt hardcover)
20 19 18 17 16 15 14 13 12 11 10 9 8

ISBN 978-0-312-37138-8 (Square Fish paperback)
20 19 18 17 16 15 14 13 12 11 10 9

The First Day of Winter

Denise Fleming

SQUARE
FISH

Henry Holt and Company ● New York

On the **first** day of winter

my best friend gave to me...

...a red cap with a gold snap.

On the **second** day of winter
my best friend gave to me
2 bright blue mittens
and a red cap with a gold snap.

On the **third** day of winter
my best friend gave to me
3 striped scarves,
2 bright blue mittens,
and a red cap with a gold snap.

On the **fourth** day of winter
my best friend gave to me
4 prickly pinecones,
3 striped scarves,
2 bright blue mittens,
and a red cap
with a gold snap.

On the **fifth** day of winter
my best friend gave to me
5 birdseed pockets,
4 prickly pinecones,
3 striped scarves,
2 bright blue mittens,
and a red cap with a gold snap.

On the **sixth** day of winter
my best friend gave to me
6 tiny twigs,
5 birdseed pockets,
4 prickly pinecones,
3 striped scarves,
2 bright blue mittens,
and a red cap
with a gold snap.

On the **seventh** day of winter

my best friend gave to me

7 maple leaves,

6 tiny twigs,

5 birdseed pockets,

4 prickly pinecones,

3 striped scarves,

2 bright blue mittens,

and a red cap with a gold snap.

On the **eighth** day of winter
my best friend gave to me
8 orange berries,
7 maple leaves,
6 tiny twigs,
5 birdseed pockets,
4 prickly pinecones,
3 striped scarves,
2 bright blue mittens,
and a red cap with a gold snap.

On the **ninth** day of winter
my best friend gave to me
9 big black buttons,
8 orange berries,
7 maple leaves,
6 tiny twigs,
5 birdseed pockets,
4 prickly pinecones,
3 striped scarves,
2 bright blue mittens,
and a red cap
with a gold snap.

On the **tenth** day of winter
my best friend gave to me
10 salty peanuts,
9 big black buttons,
8 orange berries,
7 maple leaves,
6 tiny twigs,
5 birdseed pockets,
4 prickly pinecones,
3 striped scarves,
2 bright blue mittens,
and a red cap
with a gold snap!